YOUR SUCCESS STORY

Sergio Cappelli

Dear Diana

The Queen's letter

EDIZIONI&100®
Marketing

Title: Dear Diana. The Queen's letter
Author: Sergio Cappelli
Publisher: Alessandro Gian Maria Ferri
Editorial Director: Lisa Ferri
Curator: Claudia Ferri
Editors: Andrea Brunori, Gianluigi Cervellino
Cover design: Gabriele Ponti
Website: https://edizionie100.com/
ISBN code: 979-12-81549-21-0

Edizioni &100 S.R.L., Rome
First edition Edizioni &100 Marketing - Your success story.
September 2023

Edizioni &100 Marketing, founded on December 17th, 2020 in Rome, is a publishing house that exclusively creates bespoke books to increase the personal branding and authority of **entrepreneurs** and **professionals** who wish to invest in a high-quality product that can make them *undisputed experts* in their field, and not only that...
We create meticulously crafted business books, from the first to the last page, with the aim of positively enhancing the professional image of our authors and providing them with unparalleled marketing strategies, market recognition, business development, and increased clientele.

The book has proven to be the new number one marketing tool, capable of putting on paper the personal and professional story of each professional and, at the same time, transmitting the added values, professionalism, uniqueness, and reliability of those who create it. Edizioni &100 Marketing, thanks to its team of experts, creates precise and captivating business books in less than 8 hours, taKing care of every single step, from the initial structure to the writing of the chapters, from meticulous editing to meticulous layout design, from internal graphics to attractive cover design.

Moreover, when combined with other well-executed marketing tools, the book becomes a hundred times more effective than usual. For this very reason, Edizioni &100 Marketing takes care of its authors' image from all angles, strengthening their personal branding. We create tailor-made marketing strategies, based on the author's specific needs. Our services include creating eye-catching business cards, complete with QR codes that link to multimedia content; creating a personalized website capable of detailing the main information that the author wants to share, along with engaging and explanatory photos; creating and publishing social media posts, complete with graphics and copy, for all social media platforms, and much more!

What are you waiting for? Contact Edizioni &100 Marketing to positively transform your career!

"Authority forgets a dying King."

Lord Alfred Tennyson

Diana,

people's princess,
I begin by addressing you with the title you have been given not by sovereign investiture, but by those who have loved and understood you the most.
This belated and certainly unexpected letter arises from a new feeling that has been enveloping my heart lately, and which as a Queen, but especially as a mother and grandmother, I cannot refrain from expressing.
For the Queen has a heart, and often a troubled one at that, although in the very days when the whole world mourned your passing - perhaps the most terrible days of my life - many believed that it was made of stone. They were wrong, but I cannot blame them.

Never complain, never explain.
I was taught that one must show their intellect - assuming one has an intellect worthy of attention - more than their soul, and it is as a result of this excess - or defect - of education that I sometimes conceal from myself, extinguishing it before it can ignite, any emotion capable of creating awkwardness to the Queen, and embarrassment to her interlocutors, or capable of disturbing my motionless image, imprinted for future memory on the stamps of the United Kingdom.

Why am I writing this letter to you, of all people?

Why, it would be legitimate to ask, address it to such a special recipient, who by utmost privilege or inequitable injustice is in such a higher position, than the nearly 100-year-old sender of the epistle, that she has no authority to answer, and perhaps not even to listen, to the Queen's last speech?
No, I don't think mine will be a speech. Nor the last, if I have inherited, as they say, my mother's genes.
It may be a confession, though, the first and the last, rendered not to God, but to the judgment of posterity.
But I hope that the years, though they be many, are not yet too many to make me abandon that form of caution, coupled with prudent modesty, which must always be preserved - like armour in a gladiatorial arena - to save oneself from being condemned to the pillory by those who would cast the first stone without any delay, in spite of whatever burden weighs on their conscience.
Yet it might be interesting to confess to the world the thoughts, words, deeds and omissions for which the Queen has sinned - her own greatest fault.

So why you, Diana, of all people?
Why are you receiving the serene, and yet sorrowful, externalization of a woman advanced in years, who might already have both feet in the funeral pavilion of Windsor's wives, and who is suddenly feeling old?
I would like to make you part of a journey, and by talking to you, I would like to explain to myself, and to the world that is watching and will soon judge me - yes, it will - what this very long, though not infinite, time that has been handed over to the Queen has meant to her.

What it has meant to reign, and all the while also to live. And there could be no better interlocutor than one who cannot interrupt the flow of my thoughts but, if she wants to, can munificently welcome them.
And seize every longing which these thoughts contain. Diana, I owe a debt to you which is not trivial, and which it is my will to extinguish before the bell tolls for me.

I must tell you now, before any misunderstanding can occur.
I address you as a woman, as I might only have done a few times, and as a mother. I address you, the mother of my grandchildren William and Harry, but I am the Queen, and even if I should no longer lay on my head our glorious imperial crown, nor wield the sceptre with cross or with dove, nor spin the globe at my will in the palm of my left hand, I shall forever remain the Queen, until the last hour which God shall grant me.
Like a sentence inflicted upon me, a sentence to be served without reprieve or shortcut, or a tribute rendered to me, to be honoured to the end of my strength, I remain in my place, mindful that I was anointed with holy oil by the Archbishop of Canterbury, and that I took an oath to uphold the justice and laws of my Kingdom, and to uphold our faith.
Even if I abdicated, but it will not happen, and it could not happen, I would not cease to be the Queen.

And how could it be otherwise?

To find out at almost a hundred years of age what the course of life would have been like without the load of a crown so heavy that if you don't keep your neck straight it may very well fall on you, without the Tuesday afternoons deputed to watch over the intemperance of the prime minister in office, who by elective disgrace might even be an iron lady, and without the corgis who by heraldic pride are friendly exclusively to the current Queen.

And what a misfortune to have a single date of birth, instead of the Queen's canonical two genethliacs!

I apologize, the Queen prefers not to know. And Elizabeth does not contradict her.

So you will have the delicacy to understand that I am forbidden to open my heart, in full freedom, as if I were just a common baroness – do not smile, I think you are aware that any reference is not purely coincidental.

They would say that I have lost my mind, if I would only express half the thoughts that run through my head in these hours, since I determined to add a new chapter to my biography.

I can already picture the Wikipedia paragraph, "Letter from the Queen to the ghost of her former daughter-in-law", and what the experts in *Elizabethology*, a subject in which I am supposed to excel, will invent about it.

I refer to the first Elizabeth, who died a virgin after many acts of cruelty and few good deeds, not to myself, who bore four children, but at sunset found I knew little about life, and even less about my own.

In the most desirable of conjectures they will speculate a *coup de théâtre*, the usual strategic move advised to the Queen, who for the sake of the monarchy cannot escape yet another stunt by one Blair or another.
But this time Blair has nothing to do with it, no one has solicited this letter from me, and no one knows that, albeit metaphorically, I have picked up a pen and a white sheet of paper.
Instead I am dictating, and as my thoughts appear on the tablet screen I wonder, not without understandable apprehension: what will the sequel of this story be?

Diana, I think it's the first time since the moment I have stopped filling notebooks with sticks that I am actually improvising, with not even a plot to follow or a prompter behind the scenes. It is an almost unreal condition, where the term unreal can be understood to have two different meanings, and both are right. You cannot know this feeling of freedom it gives me, entirely unknown to me, almost an intoxication that no gin and tonic has ever been up to the task of providing.
The Queen's Speech, which I read every year, and each time with more weariness and more condescension, even that speech is far from my own work.
It is not the monarch who writes it - until a few years ago on a goatskin parchment - but the prime minister, with the help of their cabinet.
If I suddenly decided to say anything else, they would probably pretend not to understand, or if cornered, they would proclaim me Elizabeth the Madwoman.

With no time to spare and with the *placet*, or more likely the whimper, of Charles, regent at last, and a few dutiful swoons from Camilla.
Her dog walker ready to administer her salts.
There has been no shortage of crazy people, neither among the Kings of England, nor among my snake-like relatives, or terrible ancestors.

But I am not crazy, and unfortunately I am also sober.
But there has been something within me lately that drives me to dare.
I think it happens to everyone.
It happened to the great Victoria, and it happened to Philip, and I could not avoid it myself.
The moment when we suddenly realize that time is short.
Even for the everlasting Queen.
And then there is less room for the bows of the Grand Chamberlain, and for sister-in-law quarrels, and daughters-in-law and know-it-all nieces, not all of them well-born, aspiring to the Olympus of first ladies, not otherwise identified, One must do what little one can still do.

Oh, Diana, you may not know this, but that night, taking your breath away, fate also uprooted the revolutionary plant that takes root in the remnants of a vitality which fades every day but cries out to be quenched, and rebels at the thought of not embellishing with an extreme bud the last babblings of life.
In other words, the improvement before the end.

So, let us begin.

There were three moments, but I might say three "calls," in my not so short existence, when I felt fully, as they were being fulfilled, that if for some reason - which would now appear to me indecipherable - I had declined to answer my life would have faltered, and I would no longer have deserved nor endured the honour and burden of the Crown.

It was not the morning of the coronation, arranged with Churchill for June the 2nd, so as not to get in the way of the Epsom derby, scheduled for a few days later, which neither of us wanted to give up; it was not the religious rite of marriage to the man I loved, and would love forever, in spite of his rambling; nor was it Philip's death, when it seemed to me that the world was collapsing around me because there was no one left who would treat me as his equal.

Not my mother, not my sister, not Philip.

Without the reverential awe that is due to the Sovereign from a subject of Her Majesty, who will have to wait until they celebrate their 100th birthday to receive the long-awaited congratulatory telegram from Buckingham Palace.

Without the natural awe of a child towards their mother, even more so if instead of telling them fairy tales where there would never be a shortage of Kings and Queens who lived happily ever after, she has spent her whole life enacting her own fairytale, in the stiff-upper-lip role of Elizabeth, forever the second, in observance of the unreversible order of the odious Roman numeration. And without the distance, if only for age reasons, to the grandmother, sovereign by accident, of a granddaughter with piercings - but being called Zara she is allowed any extravagance - of your son Harry who was filmed nude during a party in Las Vegas and managing so well not to embarrass us that he deserves my compliments, and of two other granddaughters who exchange the tiny hats of Cinderella's stepsisters, without deciding who will be Anastasia and who Drizella.

For the big day of the coronation I had prepared myself for weeks.
I walked the corridors of the Palace balancing the crown, to get used to the idea that I was Her Majesty made of blood, and I had to wear that monument on my head, even at the risk of my hairdo, like any lady sports her feathered hat at Ascot.
"Are you nervous?" My nanny Marion Crawford had asked as I prepared for the ceremony, but, changing the subject, I was pleased to reply promptly: "I think my horse will win the race in the end".
In truth, I had been preparing for *my* race from the moment our father had become King, and my sister Margaret told me I was a goner, posing as a lady of charity as she would always would, even to herself, and my mother swore eternal enmity for that scheming American who successfully imitated her in London's aristocratic salons, that Simpson who would never set

foot in England again, for it was she and she alone who was the cause of all the turmoil in our lives.
Come to think of it, without Simpson I would never have made it onto the throne.
That bag of bones who saw the light in Baltimore changed the destiny of the Kingdom more than the Virgin Queen and more than the Great-Grandmother of Europe, handing the crown over to the longest-serving sovereign in English history. And that would be me.
That's quite a lot. I don't really know if I should be grateful, but I guess I am supposed to be.

I went to the altar knowing I was taking the step I had to, and even though I was thrilled and my heart was about to burst it didn't feel like I was answering any calling.
I was very young, and I thought I had many years ahead of me as a crown princess.
And anyway everything had happened earlier, much earlier, the day Philip had appeared to me on the road to Dartmouth and I had fallen at the sight of him.

But then when Philip died I felt like something terrible and inescapable had happened, something which could in no way be averted, and which Philip and I had thought about many times, clinging to one another like lovers still, even though a lot of water had passed under the bridge.

We promised each other that the mourning would be brief, because we had to set an example for the Firm, proving that life is stronger than any absence, even that of a lifelong companion.
And life must be celebrated, without wasting unnecessary time shedding tears and wiping eyes.
In truth, I believe that neither Philip nor I wished to devote ourselves to too meagre an existence, in the absence of our other half.
The Duke of Edinburgh, in the unfortunate circumstance that I preceded him - but this eventuality was never seriously considered - would not have renounced his close conversations with aliens and his unconditional monarchical faith in butterflies, especially the blue ones, nor his carriage rides with the patient Penelope and with our granddaughter Lady Louise, and I would not have renounced my walks with Emma, my online classes in history and philosophy - top secret to all but Philip - or the children's playful smiles, and the satisfaction that one of my purebreds arriving at the finishing line can give me.
In short, we absolved each other of condolence visits.
We would not repeat the mistake of the great Victoria, with that mourning *sine die* that saddened an empire and darkened an era, no, no, no, we both protested.
As we raised our glasses, toasting to "None of us will live forever", with an unusually solemn expression in our eyes before bursting into hearty laughter, we realised that the sun was setting upon Balmoral.

Have I ever told you how I fell in love with Philip?

They say our meeting sprang from a ruse of Uncle Dickie's and it seems likely, knowing his affection for us both and his boundless ambition to conquer kingdoms for his family, but if so, then I think the Viceroy that day was inspired by God.

I was immediately enchanted by the Viking-like nature of that 18-year-old, who was so different from the young men whom I had been allowed to meet up to that point. Philip flaunted his confidence and he was extremely outgoing, but also rough and at times distant, he had a nonchalance that he declared in his every gesture and word, as if nothing directly concerned him at all.

It was precisely this enviable "distraction" of his, combined with his charm, more like that of a surly sea dog than a dignified country gentleman, that made him in my eyes - "a distant cousin without art or part", as Crawfie told me as soon as his figure disappeared over the horizon - look more like a Greek god to be worshipped than the most irresistible of Eton students, to be written off at the first skirmish with that 18-year-old, fresh from the cold showers at Gordonstoun School.

There was a moment, and the memory is as clear as if it happened yesterday, when it became obvious to me that this happy prince, who had come from afar, contained within himself all the strength I would need to become a good Queen.

I was frightened.

I was looking within myself for the magnitude, which would be needed in due time, to appear equal to the wisdom of Solomon, who had been anointed King by Zadok the priest and Nathan the prophet, but no matter

how much I indulged in searching among my small virtues, I felt inwardly and outwardly devoid of any "greatness".
I felt that day beyond any reasonable doubt, that that seaman, half-Greek and half-Danish, who had appeared to me without warning on that sunny afternoon would be the good wind I had been waiting for to start sailing on the high seas.
That evening in my bed, with the confidence in what's to come that only a thirteen-year-old girl who does not know the whims of the heart and is not afraid of the tricks of fate, I decided that Philip would marry me.
And suddenly the future seemed more bearable, even bright, despite that hat bristling with precious stones and tiny sharp, thorn-like fragments, which in our language is called the Crown.
I fell asleep with this certainty, and the next day I wrote a letter.
Then, just as it is now, no one helped me find the right words.
They flowed from the heart at the speed of light.
I would not have allowed anyone, and certainly not my sister or my mother, to suggest a single line to me.
Not even the King.

That was the first time I heard the call.
The second time was when I learned of my father's death, while I stayed in a house resting on the branches of an ancient fig tree, in a country thousands of miles away from my own.
I could have wept.

The man who loved me most on Earth had been taken from me at least ten years earlier than the stars predicted, and the government forecast, and that, for a daughter, is something intolerable.
No one, not even Prime Minister Churchill, had paternally endeavoured to prepare me for the worst, since it did not concern the health of my horses.
I would have wanted to give in to grief, for not having been there for him at the moment of his passing. If only I could have shaken his hand, I thought, feeling the relief I would have drawn from that simple gesture.
Would history books have recorded his last words?
Historians, or so-called historians, always know them, as if they were assisting the dying man in his final hour, or stealing his final confessions, hiding and eavesdropping in who knows what corner of the room, and they never fail to enunciate them, as if history could change its course according to the half-sentences said or barely sighed *in articulo mortis* by its protagonists, great or not so great.
Victoria pronounced the name Bertie, and we will never know whether it was the consort who had been waiting for her in Heaven for a long time, or the son who had been longing for her departure for as many years on Earth.
Edward VII inquired about the outcome of the horse races before closing his eyes forever.
My grandfather George V cursed his nurse, who was injecting into his veins a cocktail of cocaine and morphine so that he would pass away in time for the morning papers to give the fatal news at dawn.

Had my father named Lilibet, the daughter who had made him proud?
Or had he invoked the name of Margaret, the daughter who had given him his most cheerful moments?
My discomfort lasted only a moment, for soon after I took note that I was the new Sovereign, and I would not disappoint my father by disregarding his wishes or betraying his expectations.
I was no longer Lilibet, and I would soon forget that teenager who pretended to be a pony so as not to answer the nanny's or her mother's scolding, or that girl in love who danced at the Saddle Club in Malta with the most charming man of the Old World, tricking herself into thinking that life itself was a dance.
I knew perfectly well the speech I had read from South Africa, on the radio on 21 April 1947, at the express wish of the King.
From the Government House in Cape Town, on my 21st birthday.
That magnetic and resounding speech, according to the experts, was unanimously acclaimed both in and outside the United Kingdom.
Even the icy Queen Mary complimented me, pretending to believe it was my own doing.
The common people appreciated the emotion of a young princess, who was not addressing the subjects of the Empire, but the members of a large family.
"I declare before you all that my whole life, whether it be long or short, shall be devoted to your service and the service of our great imperial family to which we all belong".

I had to prove to the Queen of England who lived in me that that gentleman of the printed page, who corresponded to the name of Dermot Morrah, had not fallen into error handing over such a heavy obligation to fulfil to a small woman, still with so many dreams and no experience of real life.
On the 31st of January, contrary to the doctors' advice, the King wished to accompany me to the airport to say goodbye to Philip and me.
We had no idea that it was to be our last farewell.
So that morning when Philip came looking for me, his face pale, and I, descending from the tree on which I was standing, scanning the horizon, learned that the King had died, I understood then that the hour had struck.
It was the 6th of February, 1952.
Since that day, I have never retracted the words of that first speech, the speech of the future Queen.
And I have acted, and still act, in total compliance with it.

And now something about you, Diana.
They woke us up in the middle of the night.
Then, another phone call informed us that there was nothing more left to hope for.
We were stunned, incredulous, grieving.
Even though I was so angry with you, you were still a creature of God, admirable in many ways, and you were the mother of my grandchildren.
How could they believe that all of this left me indifferent?

The harsh judgement of the people and their feelings against the Queen, in those days were still a bleeding wound.
The need to protect the children prevailed over the pain. You were a loving, attentive mother, more present than I had been with Charles, Anne, Andrew and Edward. Generous with hugs and kisses.
We feared their reaction, and Philip and I joined in trying to give the boys the perception, which had to become a certainty, that they were not alone in this terrible tragedy that had struck them. That it had affected us too. We succeeded in part, or at least we thought we did.
We wove a web around them that, enveloping them, could shelter them, and in our own way we succeeded, Philip with his barbecues and his parables - an apostle of the stormy seas - and I watching them closely, like a lioness with her cubs in the wilderness.
Everything that happened in those days, that passed without time flowing, is shrouded in a grey cloud.
Yet, they are engraved in my mind.
I could tell you something of those agitated hours, I could tell you about William and Harry, and the abyss in which they found themselves, and reveal some secret to you.
But I would not tell you anything that you as a mother do not already know.

Some mistakes were made.
On my part, one, the greatest mistake of all.

I thought, and for this I suffered, that it was now dead the betrayed bride of the Prince of Wales, the mother of the future King of England, and the wounded woman of the heir to the throne, who had conceived and delivered his two sons, and I thought that this was horrible, and unjust.

But I had not considered the reaction of the people: I had measured our own grief but not the emptiness, the despair even, that your disappearance had caused in the United Kingdom and, and this is what surprised me the most, in the whole world.

I thought that the Princess of Wales had been killed, but the person who had died, that night in Paris, in that damned Pont de L'Alma tunnel, was actually the people's princess.

I cannot deny it, I felt a pang of disappointment at that badge of honour, awarded *motu proprio* by the common people to the memory of a life that had not been common.

I did not understand the meaning of that almost insulting mourning, and I wondered where the composure of the British people had gone.

One should mourn one's own dead, I thought.

Why do they not save their tears for their loved ones, for when the dreaded hour of parting comes?

It was an inexcusable mistake – which would have cost a general his victory on the battlefield - not to have grasped, through my inadequacy, that you had entered into so many hearts, and long since for those people, now in silent procession towards your home, you were a part of the closest circle of their family affections.

And that sometimes grief can unite, I did not know.
I believed that the unstoppable joy at the end of a conflict which had affected nations all over the world, could contain the unifying substance between old and new generations, between colonels and soldiers, between former fighters and war orphans, between the masses of workers and men seeking employment, between religions, races, and even between the first and the last.
But I did not know that even pain can open a gap, can provoke a spark, or grant a respite.
I apologise for that.
I stood by, incredulous.
Until someone called me back to my role as Queen.
Not that I had abdicated my duties, but I did not think that tears were part of the duties of a sovereign.
In fact I thought exactly the opposite.
What comes next is well known, my gaze fixed on the camera during the address to the nation, live from the Chinese Room at Buckingham Palace, a string of pearls around my neck, my glasses on, wearing a black dress.
But that's not all. Do you remember that display of flowers in front of the gate of Kensington Palace?
Can you remember it?
We decided to offer ourselves to public ridicule, Philip and I.
At the edge of that fragrant, seemingly endless blanket, to pay homage to your shattered life.
And to implore, without begging, a reconciliation with your people.

I did not think that that meadow of roses, mimosas, anemones, daisies, fertilised by the weeping of the people, would, in more ways than one, change my life.
The lapidation which we feared did not take place, and I was humbled and enlightened by how much love you had sown.
During that week I had been attacked, and I felt an ill-concealed unease, verging on resentment, that I harboured in the depths of my troubled soul but concealed from most, and especially from the Queen.
Those flowers and candles unsuspectedly pointed me towards a turning point, one I had probably been seeking for some time, presenting me with the face of a people I did not know in depth, in a melting pot of emotions from which I thought I had been dispensed at birth, *jure sanguinis*.
I was wrong.
I finally felt around me a thirst and hunger for love that until that afternoon were concealed to me.
I thought that if the half-masted flag had been hoisted for me, there would not have been as much participation, nor as heartfelt. It would have been lacked that feeling of afflatus which I now felt tangible, and which made me uneasy.
You were England's Rose, I was only the Queen.
Your exit from the scene, while it provoked in me a feeling of defeat which I never would have wished to know, compelled me to an examination of my present, and to an awareness which was not in my plans at all.
At least not for the current year.

The crown, though not physically on my head, had never been so heavy.

It was when a little girl stretched out her arm and offered me a bouquet of flowers that something happened.
"Do you want me to place it for you?" I asked her.
She gracefully replied that the flowers were for me.
I smiled at her, expressing my surprise.
I felt relieved, for those daisies were a kind gesture, but I did not think I deserved them.
It was then that it happened for the third time, as it had at the Dartmouth Naval Academy when I was dazzled by the wild nature of that homeless boy called Philip, and as it had happened at the Treetops Hotel in Aberdare National Park, when the flight of a golden eagle anticipated me at dawn that in another part of the world I was already seated on a throne. Now it happened in front of that blooming hill, raised for you by a human chain of uplifting love, and for the third time I decided in a beat that it was time to change course, and fly higher.

You were little more than a child when we led you senselessly towards an altar and a destiny that did not belong to you.
But wisdom comes later, and you don't have to sit on a throne to learn it.
We hoped that on that day a great love story would begin.
It happens, sometimes, that love comes later.
And I am sure that Charles wanted it badly.

You were already in love, but with a prince charming who did not exist.
That morning in St. Paul's Cathedral you were beautiful. Yet, I was startled for a moment, filled with doubt that we were making a mistake that would weigh on us all more than we could have imagined.
I had an epiphany that put off the smile on my face as I entered the church on your father's arm and you turned to me for the traditional reverence that the future Queen who will one day reign, performs before the Queen who already reigns.
You were a Spencer, you are a Spencer, and your curtsy could only be the testimony of centuries of history, and of profitable association with power.
But I was struck by the expression on your face as I realised how clueless you were, and how serenely unaware of the trap that history was playing on you, and of the trick that fate had set for you.
You were going to marry the Prince of Wales, but you had no idea, not even remotely, how steep a climb you were about to make.
In Earl Spencer's place, I would have invited you to think again, I would have begged you, all the way down the aisle of the church, to ponder your steps well, for you were still in time to escape that double somersault, too reckless for a country girl who had conquered the city by earning a living as a kindergarten teacher, without any familiarity with the poisons of the Palace.
The Crown's history has suffered other and more serious outrages, and if I had run away in a fit of panic, as well as leaving everyone cheerfully stunned, Charles

would have breathed a sigh of relief, someone would have whined or something, and you wouldn't even have been beheaded.

But it could not be, the fairytale had to go on.

How you ended up being Princess of Wales, now, almost half a century later, I do not remember.

They say the two grandmothers colluded for the nuptial conspiracy.

At Charles' first invitation for a concert at the Royal Albert Hall, Lady Fermoy accompanied you.

You had a beautiful name, more English than ours, as you never disdained to remind us as soon as the opportunity arose to do so with elegance. You had a beautiful name, you were a virgin, and you were beautiful like a rose about to bloom.

But all this cannot be enough to persuade a 20th-century maiden to marry, with so much ado about nothing.

And to have her life ruled with a sceptre as if it were a magic wand.

And it is not enough to be a good Queen.

To ascend the throne presupposes an act of will and absolute dedication.

And so I imagine they let you believe that you had entered a fairytale, thanks to the fairy godmother's gift or, who knows, maybe thanks to a kiss given to you in a dream that you could not remember once you woke up.

It took little for you to fall in love with Charles, and for him to fall in love with your naiveté.

So much so that he believed he could actually love you.

I was against this 19th century kind of marriage, which could not appear indissoluble on the threshold of the year two thousand. And then it seemed to me that you still had to play with your dolls, in Althorp's toy room, and chase your brothers in the grove adjacent to the house, taking your next steps in the lake with the swans. I had the memory of a shy girl, her eyes trembling, perpetually bundled up in oversize wool jumpers, engaged in a reckless quarrel with her body, even when you became an unripe but very promising lady of Prince Charming age.
Dutch, they called you at home, and it seemed more like a name for one of my corgis, so much so that I was tempted to steal it from you, but then they told me you would burst into tears, and so I did not.
One afternoon Charles told me about something which led me to change my mind about Lord Spencer's younger daughter.
Uncle Dickie had tragically died, and Charles was distraught.
"Diana met me shortly after the attack, at a hunting party and she approached me, and overcoming her reserve she told me that I had appeared ghastly to her, as I walked alone down the aisle of Westminster on the day of Mountbatten's funeral."
Then you had continued by saying: "it was the saddest thing I have ever seen. My heart ached for you, I thought you were so lonely; you should be with someone who cares for you."

As the Prince of Wales evoked this, I would say intimate, dialogue of yours for me, his voice was slightly trembling, and it seemed to me that his heart was sincerely vibrating.
I believed that a maiden capable of mastering her shyness to give her future King a caress, had to harbour a force invisible to most but very powerful, that could make her a good wife, and a great ruler.
I capitulated, if ever my opinion on the matter had counted for something.
But I committed another one of the mistakes that litter our relationship.
I should have met with you and explained to you the lies and truths, not let them confine you to Clarence House for protocol lessons with an octogenarian lady-in-waiting, sympathetically devoted to alcohol and too faded to teach you anything you didn't already know.
Above all, I did not take the trouble to tell you that marrying a future King does not necessarily include the right to happiness.
For a long time I did not value people's happiness and their non-negotiable right to seek a vocation to be in the world, believing that satisfaction for the fulfilment of one's duty already contained the reward and the compensation for the sacrifice made.
I observed my day going on in an admirable balance between dynastic intransigence and family discipline, and I thought that for each of us it was not difficult to put the *raison d'état* before the pangs of the heart, which only last a few seasons.

And they affect two lives - sometimes, unfortunately, three.
I underestimated that to perform one's duty daily one must have, in addition to an aptitude to employ, a strength to assert.
And temperament inevitably hardens by exercising feelings.
Even at the cost of pain.
I have asked of others a sacrifice that I myself would not have been able to make.
After that day at Dartmouth, when I was thunderstruck by the prince with sun-coloured hair who would become my irreplaceable rock, I cannot imagine my response if I had been asked to stop daydreaming about his golden locks.
But I can imagine the prostration into which I would have fallen.
If the Duke of Edinburgh had not been tenaciously clinging to my life, and fiercely present in all of ours, I would not have been the Queen you know, whom you may not have loved, but who is worthy of occupying her place, today as yesterday. If he had not been there, we would all be poorer for it.
Today that I live in a time when every dawn, besides being an Epiphany-like gift, is also a happy and uncertain bet, I have dropped many of my unshakable opinions.
And I find myself being stricter towards myself, and less intransigent towards the Queen.

We have moved through the 20th century, not the time when Kings went to meet their destiny, cleansed by the sacrament of baptism of any illusion of happiness.
Queen Mary was born in a time where the Crown Jewels could fill the void of family joys, and of an existence to be spent in the full service of Kingship, without either hope or despair, for both hope and discouragement at its absence were feelings dissonant with the serenity of Kings.
She became a kleptomaniac, but was never happy.

Would that have been possible for me?
I don't think so, although I have often put my heart into hibernation, believing I had to silence the unroyal noise of its beats.
But when I was afraid that Philip was drifting away from me, then the feelings all surfaced, and I fought like any woman offended in her feminine pride to bring him back to me.
Once, if my mind doesn't play tricks on me, I tossed my tennis racket at his head right in front of a swarm of incredulous photographers, in defiance of any royalty which would have required me to knock on the consort's door, intimating: “Open up, it's the Queen Bee.”
I feel even more guilty then.
I think of my sister Margaret.
When there were no Beatles who would have taken twenty-five seconds to say that Her Majesty is "a pretty nice girl" who "doesn't have a lot to say" - but I named them baronets, because the Queen doesn't pay attention to the words of songs - Mary Quant's miniskirt wasn't

raging, and Man hadn't set his first foot on the moon, and it seemed that princesses didn't fall in love, or if they did, no one would be allowed to spy on their smiles - whether they were brief or merry.
Their condition, like a hereditary tare, invested them with the posh dignity of a veil which made them invisible and sad.
A mendacious *raison d'état* lurked, a dragon devouring the royals, forcing them into mediocre lives void of any passion.
But then sometimes, because of a speck of dust, the irreparable happens.
So it was that while everyone let Margaret believe that the monarchy would not withstand a new shake-up, only twenty years after the Wallis Simpson cataclysm, I did not resolve to act.
I should have shrugged the crown off just for one hour, and I should have talked to her on a quiet October afternoon, big sister to little sister, over our cups of tea. And implore her to follow her sorrows, lest her breath, exhaled with unusual intimacy on that speck of dust fallen from the firmament on Captain Townsend's uniform, by some heavenly design would become a breath to his pierced heart.
Instead, I washed my hands of it, like Pontius Pilate.
The monarchy would have held on and the world would have rejoiced, taking the side of the dream, and the Crown would have emerged glowing from that bold choice, aimed at the future of the third millennium which was preparing to knock on our doors.

But above all, Margaret would have aligned her destiny with her lucky star.
Making amends now counts for little.

And what about Charles? What about you?
We believed it was enough to boast a few William the Conquerors in our common family tree, and neighbouring properties, and a good relationship, and two kindred, if not identical, upbringings with friendly grandmothers who would have watched over you - instead they deftly stole your more or less green years so that you could live happily ever after, in the fairytale we had sewn for you.
Without having the flair of the Brothers Grimm.

Too bad there was no happy ending.
You resented the Scottish rain, the horses, the dogs, the hunting trips, the hours Charles spent fishing, the time he spent reading.
While Charles could not get over how much you enjoyed, and were finally at ease, being among suffering people, undernourished children and underprivileged beings in general.
Except if you were twirling around for fifteen overwhelming minutes with that actor with the Saturday night fever.
Ah Travolta, on the eve of my own funeral - which will be more impressive than that of any Hollywood star - I can finally say it, I never liked that Oscar night kind of guy.

And it's a pity that at the White House, after that dance, more like that of a cheerleader than of a princess of Wales, nobody remembers that with you was also the future King of England.

And yet thank you, Diana.

For having had more courage than the rest of us.

For deciding not to submit, for rebelling, for clumsily succumbing to the temptation to be happy.

Those who are more realists than royals can be still believe that you had to sacrifice yourself, subordinate your rights as a woman to your duties as a future Queen, and I used to believe it along with them.

I wondered how you could act following the model of any middle class girl, when you should by birth have nurtured an absolute deference to the sacredness of the mandate which had been conferred on you in St. Paul's Cathedral.

I thought, and I could not absolve you, that you were kicking away eternity, not wishing to come to terms with the trivial rivalry between a rottweiler, not of immaculate pedigree, and a cow gone mad with love - I beg your pardon but the onomastics are not inspiring me - in a public fight for the exclusive on a prince so bloodthirsty that he not too secretly dreamed of turning into a tampon.

I was furious, and how could I not be?

Today, in the pensive state where I finally relegated myself, I believe you had no obligation to the Crown, to the Prince of Wales, or to the Nation, nor the obligation to sacrifice your life.

And I thank you for not doing it.

We had destined you to be the Queen of England but the twists and turns of life and above all the intention, even more than the will, that underlay your every action and drove it in one direction and not another plotted for you, crowning you Queen of Hearts.
You could have embraced your subjects but you chose to embrace the men and women of the world.
During these years even more than when you were alive - for then I was busy parrying the blows inflicted on the monarchy by your disgraceful deeds - but afterwards, when I tried to measure myself against your stature as a woman, and no longer as a royal highness, I sincerely admired you.
Do you know why?
You received as a gift a precious and uncommon talent, the ability to be in the world truly loving your neighbour. While I had to continually appeal to my sense of duty, seeking within me an ever fertile feeling of responsibility towards the nation, you had a mine to dig into, immeasurably greater, possibly inexhaustible, which was your heart.
I have watched you lead Mother Teresa by the hand, tall and elegant, but perfectly at ease with that saint of poverty, and she with you, like two sisters separated at birth yet indissolubly united by a commonality of purpose.
To whisper words of love into the ear of that little nun, immense in her white sari, you had to bend, but neither you nor she lost your original beauty.

I have seen you hold AIDS patients to your breast with the same affection with which you held your children, I have seen you kiss lepers and walk through a minefield like a fighter armed only with agape.
I could not have done it, I could not do it, and now that the end is near I can say I did not do it.

Dear Diana, you could not carry the people to a more just world, but you performed a revolutionary action on behalf of millions of women.
To take note of this mortifies my person and diminishes my work.
Not because of your light, which even after a quarter of a century shines brighter than ever.
But because I lacked the royalty that could interpret, stripped of its symbols and devoid of all arrogance, the aspiration of a woman to be recognized, not unlike any other human creature.
Instead of shining as you shone, I remained opaque.

Have I now become dull?
Have old age, and the death of my companion, taken away the light of my reason?
Far from it. Never before have I seen so far, and so clearly.
When, after your interview, which may have been taken from you under false pretences, but frankly I don't give a hoot, I wrote to Charles demanding that he ask for a divorce. Philip did not agree.

I believe I saved the image of the future King, and gave you a golden key to get out of a cage which was anything but golden.
It did not take you long to break the chains, and so you took flight.
A flight that, alas, was unexpectedly short.

Philip loved you.
In his own way, of course, but I never heard him rail against you as he used to do towards Sarah, not even when you challenged our self-control and his aplomb, more British than mine.
Not only did he love you, but he respected your eagerness to expand, and found in you his own estrangement from the rules.
When he began writing to you, always in his own hand, those letters were important to him.
You addressed him as "dear pa".
And he felt invested with a task that he wanted to perform with the utmost seriousness and honesty.
Frankness was among his best qualities.
He was very sorry when your correspondence ended.
But he never stopped taking an interest in you.
I believe you loved him and returned his affection.
In fact, I am certain of it and I remain grateful to you for it.
He was furious when he learned of Charles's betrayal with Camilla. He came to me, asking me how it was possible that a man with good sense - and good taste, he added - could prefer to you, who had youth, beauty and class, an equine woman, unattractive from her first

breath - in truth he expressed himself more strongly - and moreover married, with a husband and children, who could only kick him in bed.
Philip was like that.
I believe it was also in the name of your friendship that he offered to follow your coffin, on the day of the funeral, so as not to lose sight of the boys.
He made a commitment to them, to be with them. I never asked him what they said to each other, but he spoke incessantly to William.
I think it was a great act of love, towards your children and his grandchildren, but it was also his way, discreet and loyal, of making peace with you.
He would not have wanted you to leave without a gesture from him.

I, on the other hand, was the Queen, become by national plebiscite the most pernicious of businesswomen, a perfidious mother-in-law, and without a shred of humanity towards her daughter-in-law and her friends.
I understood that I had to perform an action which was both an act of homage to your person and a sign of peace, offered as a sacrifice by the sovereign to her subjects, the sealing of a new pact between the Crown and the people.
The gun carriage with the coffin was pulled by six horses.
The streets were closed to traffic and even air flights were diverted from London, in the supreme silence only the hooves of the horses could be heard.

When at the passing of the coffin, covered by the royal standard with an ermine border, I bowed my head. I was sincerely contrite.
In the face of death, the Queen could not help but bow.

They wrote, that that slight bending of my head, which contained both a declaration of deference and a petition, the former to the people's princess and the latter to her people, saved the Crown.
That it preserved it on my head.
It might be.

With that tribute, unexpected and not codified by protocol, I upset the cards of History, and restored to the Throne the splendour of your sanctification.
No longer the unhappy creature, banished from the royal family, but the huntress goddess, protector of all women.
With an almost imperceptible movement of the body, but with the iconic power of a genuflection, I assured the monarchy's resurrection after days of agony.
The belligerence turned into an alliance, and you, Diana, became the icon of the century, but with my blessing you also became the Joan of Arc of the United Kingdom, the champion of a different royalty, the only one you could fulfil with your heart and plead with the *impetus* of a maiden of Albion.
I, with no time to evade or to resist, unworthily but not without a dignity to represent, picked up the baton of a newborn family lexicon, originated by you, in order to

converse no longer with subjects but with my neighbour.
And so it was.

The last twenty-five years of my reign have been marked by change, and by your teachings.
With the exception of Sophie, to whom I told my secret one forgotten afternoon, in contravention of my rule not to confide in the living, no one knows that I have never lost you nor set you aside, both in my prayers and in my thoughts.
You have remained for me a candle lit in the night. Who could have believed it?
For the mistakes not to be repeated, and the inimitable genius of your life.
Your brother thundered in church - he could have been kinder, and chosen less provocative words.
"Diana was the very essence of compassion, of duty, of style, of beauty. All over the world she was a symbol of selfless humanity.... Someone with a natural nobility who was classless and who proved in the last year that she needed no royal title to continue to generate her particular brand of magic."
Yes, you had been stripped of your Royal Highness treatment, but had the ninth Earl Spencer investigated the reasons for that *deminutio*?
I felt a sense of rebellion towards that lecture against the Crown which did not consider your errors but condemned ours without possibility of appeal.

However, when asked what I thought about it, I could not help but reply: "She was your sister, and you have every right to say whatever you feel."
In the years that followed, in going back in my mind to that speech I found some illuminating passages, almost a warning to the monarchy.
And to the Queen.
"The world sensed this part of her character and cherished her for her vulnerability whilst admiring her for her honesty."
And again:
"But your greatest gift was your intuition, and it was a gift you used wisely. This is what underpinned all your other wonderful attribute."

If I had to summarise the lesson you bequeathed to us in four cardinal points, I would use four words, corresponding to as many states of mind that since you are no longer with us have accompanied me like a compass, orienting my life towards new lights, sometimes flickering and dim, sometimes shining and even dazzling. These four words are vulnerability, intuition, compassion and impermanence.
The first three were contained in your brother's speech in church.

There is no sin of pride more execrable of which a human being and even more so a monarch - can be stained, than that of not showing their wounds to the naked eye, and not letting the scars that survive the wounds remain visible as testimony and memory of having lived much and suffered as much.
You, thanks to your Achilles' heel, with the blazon of a vulnerable soul, have walked proudly in sickness and in health, for better and for worse.
It was time for me to shed that armour, I thought, an armour not unlike the carapace of a turtle, and show the truth which often languished, and sometimes agonised, under a shield of bones and vertebrae that either numbed it, drowsed it, or oppressed it to the point of suppression.
When the turtle stretches its neck, and leans towards us and squints its eyes, it is declaring its need for affection.

But a human being cannot breathe, tremble and love in the same way as a turtle does.

Intuition: the ability to look at others, name their needs, and if possible enter into their dreams.
A category of the heart.
I have belatedly begun to pay attention to the intermittences of the heart, which are often annoying interferences to the established order of our authorised biography, but hearing mine, and listening to others', has exalted with an unknown enthusiasm my daily gestures.
And it gave a new course to my reign.
So I did not consider it an affront to the Crown, or to the royals gathered to commemorate Prince Philip, to make my entrance at Westminster Abbey on Andrew's arm.
Is there not also a parable to that effect?
Why should the world blame me, I asked myself, if I wished to receive and give consolation to my neediest son, to give and receive love, even more so on that day of remembrance.
Andrew accompanied me, heavy with many springs and pained by many misfortunes, and I, in spite of his faults, entrusted myself to him, trusting in his repentance and in God's forgiveness, for the shortcomings of both.
As a sovereign, I intended to deprive him of his military titles, but as a mother I could not deprive him of the dignity of a son, inflicting on him a punishment I could not bear, for me more bitter than the pains with which I gave birth to him.

In the pitiless eyes of the world, Andrew would have lapsed, *sine nobilitate*, from the right to mourn his father. I held him close, and told him we would shed a few furtive tears together for the broken column of our lives.
They say he is my favourite and I know that a mother, as the days go by, prefers the child who has made the most mistakes.
And then the pandemic arrived.
That speech would not have been possible before Diana. I would have addressed the Country, which would have risen, bigger and stronger than before; instead, I spoke to each of the people listening to me, I went into their homes, asking permission, and for a few minutes we looked intensely into each other's eyes, and mutually promised each other that together we could make it.
That we would meet again.
You would have worn a scrub and helped the nurses, your former butler said, but your children liked the Queen's speech, and my heart rejoiced.
As a sovereign, and as a grandmother.

The third point is compassion: "Diana was the very essence of compassion", were the solemn words spoken for you with love by Earl Spencer.
There is an episode in my life as a sovereign which only a few people know, and in which I believe I was inspired by you.
David Nott, a valiant surgeon who had worked in Aleppo and had not yet overcome the trauma of that painful experience, asked to see me.

In the days leading up to our meeting, I prepared myself, imagining the questions I could ask him, without burdening his already strained sensibility.
But, when I had him in front of me, I realised that I would reach his heart more powerfully without using words.
Overcoming my natural reluctance to any form of greeting other than the ritual royal wave, I took Dr Nott's hands in mine, not without inexplicable circumspection, and gratefully caressed them.
During lunch, I began to talk to him about my little quirks, and then introduced him to my corgis, who welcomed the doctor as a member of our extended family.
They seemed to feel a pang in their hearts, seeing that good man so distressed.
I told my guest their personal stories, disclosed their personal details, and feeling him share their little lives, I asked him if he would like to take some biscuits from a box, which I pointed out, to offer them something to munch on.
When he seemed reassured, I said to him:
"There, that's so much better than talking, isn't it?"
Dr Nott a few days later reassured me in a note that he had calmed down that afternoon, and that for an hour the memories of Aleppo had weighed less heavily on his distraught heart.
I had given him my attention by giving him the perception that he was a unique human being for me, worthy of my care.

Perhaps this is what compassion is, a participation in the suffering of others, with which a lump in the throat may be associated.
Is that so, Diana?

The last word that your earthly transit has given me is impermanence.
That is, the consciousness of our impermanence.
The crash of the Princess of Wales's Mercedes into the thirteenth pylon of the Alma bridge in Paris on the 31st of August 1997, chased by the paparazzi - your death, Diana - shocked the world, and put the Queen on trial.
While the inhabitants of the Earth wanted to unite in your name, and feed on the common feeling of farewell, I could not participate in this liturgy of grief.
It was enough that I did not wet my lips at that bitter chalice, for the people, who had hitherto shown respect for their sovereign, to turn against my person and against the institution I represent.
I understood, as a result of those convulsive days, the value of time that changes conditions, abruptly transforms feelings, scandalously changes destinies, and can make eternity short.
Isn't it true what Farouk said, when in 1948 he prophesized between the serious and the jesting our immortality?
It may come a day when even the King of England will disappear.
There is a pact, which can be dissolved at any time, and without any warning.
My bowing, as you passed, rebuilt the long-lost alliance.

But nothing lasts forever.

And now, before evening falls, a few more words about your children and the future Queen of the United Kingdom.
If only you knew how many times over the years I have felt like a thief.
Especially in the early days, when we surrounded William and Harry, who were so young and in dire need of all our attention, of all our care, the only balm that could soothe the sting of their wounds, but always anxious not to remove from their hearts the memory of the happy days they had lived with you, and not to lose the precious scent of your kisses that we could still feel around them, left indelibly, I know it now, by your lips on their cheeks.
Forgetting about your bond of love, mother to sons, and sons to mothers, would have been the most unjust insult to your interrupted motherhood, and the loss of an invaluable archive of feelings for William and Harry, thanks to which they were able to extend your past into a longer future.
The boys heard your name echoing in the rooms where you lived.
We did not prevent them from discovering under the stones the secret of the wellspring.
Of this, if it is possible to know things up there, you can give us credit.

Not only that, but Philip and I, when faced with the choices we had to make, constantly questioned what you would have thought of our project regarding the education of your boys.
We never forgot that one day they would become grown men, and they should not be unworthy of the flower that brought them into the world.
What else there is to say?
Then came the celebration for the 10th anniversary of your death, at London's Wembley Arena, with Elton John, opening the evening with *Candle in the wind.*
"I want this event," William told me, "to help people remember the many good and beautiful deeds of our mother."
I could only nod.
It was the birthday present William and Harry wanted for you, for the forty-six years you would have celebrated.
At the concert in your honour, first on the stage, and then in the stands, the boys were one more beautiful than the other, united in the emotion of your embrace and rejoicing in unison, with a joy that lit up their faces, equal in their truth as two drops of water, and dissimilar as are the destinies of two young men, who are finally directing their lives, each drawing a different line, supporting each other, without hindrance, along the path that awaits them, both a single gift from God.
That night, as I gave thanks to the Lord, I raised a supplication to Heaven that you might see them.

I realised how much time had passed, and that, if there ever was, no more reprobation would lodge in my heart, about your conduct, your disasters, your inconclusive attack, on the royal machine and the foundations of our family.
Only gratitude remained, for making me the grandmother - and then the substitute mother - of those two boys.
Whom I love, and I tremble in admitting it, more than my own children.

Time is man's best teacher, taught me by example if not by phrases Sir Winston Churchill, whom I considered a second father.
The most merciful teacher, but the least forgiving.

I was very close to the boys as they grew up without their mother.
Charles alone could not do it.
Your sisters helped us, and they were not the only ones.
And I have given the boys more care than I gave Charles, Anne, Andrew and Edward in their youth.
The years inevitably add wisdom, and while they take away some of our strength, they give us the opportunity to delight in the truest joys of life.
I look at them now, and William has turned forty, he has three children who bring us infinite joy, and he will be a good King, probably better than his father, certainly better than me. Harry has named his second daughter Lilibet Diana.

On this Earth, in a corner of the world, far away from our England, a little woman is growing up combining our names in one.
Is it not wonderful?
The two brothers are no longer inseparable like they were that night at Wembley.
Or like when Harry was William's best man, on the day of his marriage to Kate, and then William reciprocated, when his brother led that Meghan to the altar.
But it does not bother me, centuries of family history teach us that it happens, that it can happen.
But you know, they used to sit every morning in the same car, singing happily at the top of their lungs with you who were driving and the bodyguard, who was also singing Tina Turner tunes, all the way from home to school. And then, because that's what life is like, they have walked together through London, following the coffin of a woman who was the best and the most beloved of mothers, hearing in the silence only the sobs of the people and the footsteps of the horses on the pavement. That kind of love endures forever, there can be no opposing force capable of tearing it down or scarring it.
Love is not a stone that can crumble, but a river that flows.
The boys suffer for the distance that has come between them, and they regret it without showing it. They are proud, and have the arrogance of their age, but we need to give them time. Soon something will happen to unite them again.

I can already see them, walking side by side, and I hope I am not mistaken.
With the blessing of your love, our love, which is just as much for William as it is for Harry. Our boys.
Don't you think so, Diana?

And now for the sore spot.
If one day we will meet, as is it possible, I, who do not like to feel cornered, neither as Queen nor even less as mother-in-law, how will I face the embarrassment of Camilla being Queen?
Certainly I can imagine that the royal quarrels of this Kingdom will not be matters to be dealt within the other - that of Heaven - where I presume we shall all be common immortals, without even inquiring whether we are descended from Adam, or directly from God.
But I don't think it will be pleasant for you to know, or for me to have to be the one to inform you, to have to acknowledge that the Rottweiler has stopped snarling and has taken my place.
So I must tell you that thanks to her new hair dye the former rottweiler has been promoted to golden retriever, and this is already a step forward in favour of the future of the monarchy.
Camilla in all these years has protested a tenacious attachment to the institutions, respecting them, even at the cost of appearing resigned, even insignificant, always without showing off, and with a certain elegance, despite traits and movements that are not very feminine, nor very regal, or even very human.

In short, the new Queen will bring to the throne everything you lacked. But she will miss the stars that God with a broad gesture was pleased to distribute in your eyes. And she will be a good Queen, and at last a consort, I think that goes without saying, more circumspect than you, who would have offended the King's majesty by dancing with wolves.
Forced to move the wedding date countless times, including the last one, the one that finally declared them husband and wife, because of the Pope's funeral in Vatican City. Neither Philip nor I were present at the celebration of the rite.
I wonder if my subjects appreciated this delicacy towards you.
Now it is time for her to reign, and I wish it to be so, to ensure continuity to the Crown and give support to the King, only his mother can know how much Charles will need it.
I have observed her and she is almost an old woman, not brilliant, but witty and sometimes ironic, of average intelligence, with the right amount of human capital to be the discreet and not shrill companion of the new ruler of the United Kingdom.
When the time comes.
Besides, to her as much as to you I owe a debt of gratitude, do you know that? For never having, not even by mistake or through an occasional weakness, or in a moment of illusory omnipotence, attempted to fill the vacant role of the mother of your sons, William and Harry, by unceremoniously substituting herself to the people's princess.

I would not have allowed it, though the former evil woman does not know that, but for this too one day not far off she will wear a crown balanced on her head.

My letter to you is coming to an end, as is my pilgrimage in this Kingdom.
I expect to find another where, I hope, there will be more freedom, even for a Queen who was never a drag, but who would have loved, you know not how much, to walk along the Thames and through the streets of the world all alone, dressed as a girl.
"All my possessions for one moment of time," said the other Elizabeth on her deathbed.
Still adorned in a swollen pointed bodice, her skirt heavy, her white ruff pleated around her neck, her red wig freshly curled, she looked at herself in the mirror one last time, before parting with herself.
Even in the end, we will not look alike.
For me, when the hour strikes, it will be the right time.
I do not yearn for one more moment in the mystical body of the Queen, anointed with holy oil as the priests and prophets were anointed.
Not that I did not love, respect and reverence her.
But she was alone, she is alone.
The due time has almost come, and punctuality is the courtesy of Kings.

The 6th of February seventy years ago at Sandringham House had been a cold, but dry and sunny day.
The King, as serene and happy as he had been lately, had spent it hunting with your grandfather, Diana, his lifelong friend Lord Fermoy. On his return he had joked with his two grandchildren, eaten a frugal meal and gone

to bed, with his usual glass of chocolate liqueur on the bedside table.
At 7.30 a.m., when the valet who had served him for twenty years, James McDonald, went to wake him up, the King did not answer.
He had died in the night, without suffering.
That very morning, the 6th of February, I was in Kenya, the first stop on what was supposed to be a long tour of the Commonwealth.
I woke up very early. We were staying in an exclusive resort with wooden cottages built in the trees.
I watched from my room a fight between two rhinos and then climbed a lookout tower, ready to watch the sunrise.
With the first light of dawn a lone eagle passed through the trees, flying low over our heads.
In those same hours, thousands of miles away, in England, King George VI passed away in his sleep.
The legendary English hunter Jim Corbett, who had killed dozens of man-eating tigers around the villages of India, was also in the lodge, and wrote a sentence in the guest book: "For the first time in history, a young girl climbed a tree one day as a Princess and descended from it the following day as a Queen. May God bless her."

Since then "the world's sweetheart", as the Americans called me while I was visiting their country, has never let go.
How did I do it?

First of all by enduring, and living through seven decades of British history without ever giving in to the temptation to fake a headache and at least for once run away from something.
And being there, always, in every circumstance, whether public or private, more important or less important, was no small test, in a monarchy that reigns but does not rule, in a ruling house that was born German and became resolutely English, not without the shedding of blue blood, thanks to a reformation worthy of Luther from Hanover to Windsor, with Gotha in between them.
And then I had to read the Queen's speech, with the right accent and without any prevarication, to the people who cut off the head of their King long before their French cousins.
Every morning at my desk at half past nine, like a fastidious and somewhat pedantic office manager, I went through the state documents of the “red boxes” to get enough information to give the minister in charge a hard time, showing the same imperturbable lips whether he was a lord, a grocer's daughter, or the grandson of a RAF pilot.
On tiptoe and without extravagance, I have opposed alpha males and females among the Tories as among the Labour.
In seventy years of reign, I have never allowed the mask to slip from my face.
Responding almost to perfection to the expectations of my subjects, for whom the Queen must embody with sobriety and naturalness the eminently British attitude

of reconciling tradition and contemporaneity, of holding together everything and the opposite of everything.
A very British peculiarity, which has allowed me, I can see it now, to act as a damper on society's excessively abrupt accelerations without ever hindering them, but merely accompanying them and taking note of them.
Still in the world but at a certain distance, with the ambition to be "above" - still that imperial illusion which has not entirely faded and which perpetuates itself in that feeling of lost grandeur, which would still make us exclaim: "Fog in the Channel - continent cut off!".

It is thanks to my family's upbringing: at Buckingham Palace, during the Second World War, the royal family followed rationing like everyone else, and when the palace was bombed by the Luftwaffe my mother, who was a pragmatic woman, commented: "I'm glad we have been bombed. Now I can look the East End in the face." The East End, the working-class neighbourhood devastated by the bombs.
While others fled to safety without saving their honour, nor the lives of their subjects, we remained in our place. This is history, I did not write it. Even Margaret and I, whom Churchill wanted to send to Canada, did not move. Famous was the Queen's reply: "The children won't go without me. I won't leave the King. And the King will never leave."
On this capital of trust which I could not betray I built my Kingdom.

On my own I put in a good character and a certain temperament - not too edgy, not too haughty either - a lot of common sense and a bit of thrift, small virtues that the subjects ended up appreciating, in time and with the help of St James.
Rubber boots, trench coats and headscarves for walking on the moors, Dior and Givenchy banned at the palace balls, which I left without regrets to my idle sister and daughters-in-law. Dresses worn many times over and heels repaired, in the evenings at home bland and patriotic food, even sometimes fish and chips, with the sole concession of Béarnaise sauce, half lemons sent back to the kitchen from the table because they may still be needed, the end-of-day tour of Buckingham Palace to check the lights and turn off the last ones left carelessly on. This is how I prevented the crown from wobbling too much on my head.
As well as with a few hundred thousand telegrams to the British people, for their diamond wedding anniversaries. With the sole power to "advise, encourage, warn" I inaugurated the annual sessions of Parliament, without letting out any political convictions in public.
Moving for more than half a century in an almost improbable, and often precarious, balance between two wings of the crowd, on the one hand those who applauded me on stamps and banknotes, teacups and T-shirts, and on the other the noisy rebellion of those who demanded that we at least pay taxes, me and my tribe of royal, and sometimes debauched, freeloaders, and even now overreacting at the evidence of the expense which will have to be faced for the marathon of my funeral,

when the Prime Minister will receive the notorious dispatch saying that "London Bridge is down".
Over fourteen lustres, many heads of state, many Archbishops of Canterbury, many successors of Peter met, not to mention the theory of fourteen or fifteen heads of government, I have lost count, including the last one I will see one of these days.
I wish I could erase Tuesday from every week of the next millennium!
Margaret Thatcher, who was also a fervent royalist, and reluctantly sung my praises, was an almost impossible woman.
Even though I almost loved her in the end, when she no longer recognised me. I had bitter clashes with her. Her iron fist against the striking miners, her wall-to-wall policy... I could not accept any of it.
Leftist sympathies? No, I acted like my grandfather, the conservative George V, who, when confronted in 1926 with the intemperate tirade of Lord Durham, the coal pit owner, against "those damned revolutionaries" on strike, retorted dryly: "Try living on their wages before you judge them."
With Thatcher - yes, her again - my reactions ranged from exasperated to sarcastic. At Balmoral Castle in Scotland, where it was customary to offer guests a barbecue where Philip grilled sausages and I washed the dishes at the end, to avoid the prolongation of a conversation that would become pernicious between me and that lady with the Caligula eyes, faced with the premier's attempts to help me, I once blurted out: "Will someone tell that woman to sit down?"

The relationship with the "third way" premier Tony Blair was also rocky.
He admired you greatly, Diana, I would say immensely.
The vulgate - I don't know if this is the correct term but I can't think of a less brutal one - still thinks that the Queen did not forgive him for forcing her hand after the death of the Princess of Wales by pressing her into making a speech she did not want to make, and to attend your funeral, and to display the flag at half-mast on Buckingham Palace.
That's nonsense. He showed me a way forward, and for that I can only be grateful.
The story is more complex, and the lack of harmony between us was more of substance: I could not like his "presidential" attitude, his manners too blunt to belong to a gentleman, his decisionist simplification of rules and procedures, his considering the audiences with the Queen a mere formality.
I could not forbid him anything, but I took my revenge by not granting him, except after exhausting foreplay, the longed-for, and very erotic for him, Order of the Garter, and by not inviting him to the wedding of the Duke of Cambridge in 2011.
"Honi soit qui mal y pense!"
But since revenge is a dish best served cold, during the premier's ritual summer visit to Balmoral with his wife, I reserved the chilliest rooms in the castle for the couple.
In summer in Scotland temperatures can be very cold, and Blair and his consort Cherie, as hoped, had their teeth chattering under the sheets.

Nothing compared to the ice house where Tsarina Anna hosted the court jester and his wife, who was notoriously the ugliest woman in all of Russia, for their wedding night.
Equal treatment for jester and minister, but mine was much more magnanimous.
Apparently the side effects propitiated but unpredicted were the same - the two women both came out pregnant from the experience, the former favoured by the cold steppe which surrounded the love nest, and the latter by the cold war ongoing between her seed-bearer and the evil Queen.

The radical and anti-Windsor Tony Benn, Postmaster General under Wilson, came before me with a draft stamp which would have abolished my effigy, and left the hearing convinced he had won his petty battle.
He believed he had guillotined me, with a kind of postal "terror", bloodier than that of Robespierre.
And without even according me the ritual of the last wish.
I merely listened to him, not uttering a word or blinking, for forty interminable minutes, which I was forced to end with the silent alphabet of my bag.
My secretary, meanwhile, had already successfully contacted the premier, peremptorily demanding that the project be set aside.
Later, to those who suggested that I should compensate Benn by inviting him to the Palace, I could only reply laconically: "No, he does not like us."

Not to mention the little joke I played on Blair's deputy, the "Republican" Lord John Prescott.
I didn't come up with it on my own, not having the diplomatic skill or even the two-faced nature of the Prince of Talleyrand, but I did it with the help of an unseen strategist very devoted to me.
On one public occasion, as Prescott spoke to me, I lowered my voice more and more, reducing it to a whisper, and forcing him to bend forward, to barely grasp what I was saying.
Basically forcing him to genuflect almost to the ground, in the presence of my august person.

Once I was forced to reply to the Conservative David Cameron, who had made an hardly appropriate objection: "Her Majesty solved that problem seven ministers before you."
Silence fell.

The memories are beginning to crowd my head.
In 2018 with Prince Charles and Camilla, I had to welcome the US President and the American First Lady, making an effort to do the honours, as if it were not that guy Trump.
But I cannot deny that I was pleased when royal princess Anne, whom I called to greet them, stood in the doorway avoiding any handshake.
And we were not at the time of the covid.
What can I say? The apple doesn't fall far from the tree.

In 2003 in London I have met for the first time the reigning Tsar, in his capacity as president of the Russian Federation.
Upon seeing him, Home Secretary David Blunkett's dog barked loudly and stopped on its tracks. Blunkett apologised, but I said: "Dogs have interesting instincts, don't they?"
Should he still be at large, that Putin fellow, when the Lord will decide to call me to him, I wish he would not attend my funeral.
More than a wish, I would say it is an order from Her Majesty the Queen.
Don't you agree, Diana?

Sometimes the idea of royalty has come to my rescue.
It is said that blue is the colour to wear when you are feeling stressed, or burdened, and looking for some peace.
Cobalt blue was the shade of the dress I wore when we received at Buckingham Palace the President of the United States and his First Lady, John and Jacqueline Kennedy.
It was the 5th of June 1961 and at the age of thirty-five I had already had three children: Charles aged thirteen, Anne aged eleven and little Andrew who was one year old.
I was aware that I risked looking "dusty" and even ancient, as much as Jackie would appear contemporary, and bright.

It was for this reason that, instead of competing on style, a field where I was at risk of hurting myself, I decided to focus on what I had by divine right, and to which Jackie could not aspire: royalty.
I summoned my trusted stylist Sir Norman Bishop Hartnell and asked him for help. Hartnell designed for me a Blue Royale tulle ball gown with shoulder pads.
Wide, fairytale-like, but at the same time elegant and not too showy.
Something that only The Queen could wear with ease, without looking like Scarlett at Twelve Oaks, and that on a first lady would inevitably look out of place.
A model that Jacqueline Bouvier had dreamed of wearing, as a teenager, while fantasising about marrying Prince Charming.
Hartnell matched the dress with a pair of white satin gloves. We chose more carefully than usual the jewellery I would wear, in a triumph of diamonds and sapphires.
In the end I was perfect, I had conquered my innate reluctance to duel with another woman, and in the photos of that historic encounter, nothing about Jackie managed to overshadow me.

The Earl of Wessex arrived years later.

With Edward the brood was complete.
It was a pity that the flipside of such tenacious devotion to the Queen's profession was a family that I let grow up in a destitution of goodnight kisses.
Three out of four divorced, and some with much fanfare. First, the avant-garde trio formed by Charles, you and Camilla. Then the serial cheater Andrew and the mischievous Sarah, who was not without a number of hidden qualities, at least as many as all of her fingers, toes included. And the other triangle, more domestic and less official, between royal princess Anne, the consort elected *pro tempore* as guardian of the nuptial enclosure, and at least one of her stallions of pure equine blood.
Still better than the staff on duty. Then Andrew's latest scandal and the exit of Harry and that Meghan girl from the royal family have left their marks on the Queen.

And what about Charles?
The Prince of Wales, the future King.
He began his long career as a prince by getting a princess wrong, something no fairytale-loving subject will ever forgive him for.
Because you were a magnificent teenager, not yet in the mood for heavenly assumption, while he liked the seasoned ugly girl.

And if you have big ears - we don't know from which ancestor of his father he inherited them - then you are doomed.
Poor Charles. We never considered, Philip and I, that the solution to all his woes would be to cut off his damn ears. When his situation as heir to the throne became chronic - I would have to beat my chest and say *mea culpa* three times because of my incurable longevity - Charles was, depending on the mood of the prime ministers and of certain press, either the betrayer, the unloved son - even this infamy I had to swallow - or the divorced husband whom your death would force into a life of penance.

However, Charles went from being a toad to being a prince, and from a certain episode onwards of the TV series The Crown he stopped saying melancholic phrases, doing foolish things and feeling sorry for himself.
I hope the series was true to reality.
Having turned the fateful age of seventy, he finally got his wisdom teeth out.
Charles is now more King, and less prince on the pea.
Don't smile, I'm not referring to a valet with whom he would pleasure himself every morning while the unfortunate man smears his toothpaste - we haven't minded this kind of things in the family from Richard The Lionheart onwards - but to his laughable need to take his personal mattress with him on every trip, to avoid waking up on the verge of a nervous breakdown after a

sleepless night counting sheep on a naturally organic lawn.
I get that the British are eccentric by definition, and people like them for that too, but I explained to my eldest son that everything must always be done with measure. He still looks a bit like a whipped dog, and maybe he has some reason to feel that way: a gruff father like the Duke of Edinburgh, a less than affectionate mother - that would be me - and an ex-wife pampered by the world who tried her best to make him the most bullied Prince Charming of the 20th century.
The ex-wife, in this portrait gallery, is you.

Surrounded by characters of such stature, Charles is a survivor, one who is in danger of reaching the finishing line with too many years on his shoulders and too much oppression on his back, and yet he will get there with solidity and with a sense of purpose. He will get there with solidity, and accompanied by the woman who has finally come through for him, and for his outfits.
I could not fail to compensate Camilla, Duchess of Cornwall, for having taken care of the image of Charles, more and more in the nonchalant clothes of the Duke of Rothesay, and less and less in the worn-out ones of the Prince of Wales, thanks to an elegant kilt, the highlight of his wardrobe, and the needle of the scale between the cool green that dwells in his ego thought - I said echo, but the proofreader writes stubbornly ego - and the Great Stewart of Scotland which thrives among the fog and bagpipes of his roots.

If your Charles is no longer disliked by his subjects as he was in the age of Diana, prematurely subjected to universal prejudice, your son William and his wife Kate, on the other hand, seem to have taken the royal master's degree, with the ability to save the day.
While Harry, in spite of his nebulous origins, is the one who resembles you the most, physically the same as his grandfather, but unconventional like you, fragile and in need of love, but also in his own way a rebel, one who does not bend and yet is slowly crumbling.

I shall not go on, Diana, I would risk going over the limits imposed by the protocol of the Queen's visits to the heavenly bodies.
When one gets old, one wants to slow down time, but time does not stop. So you hold on to people.
If they are there, you are still there.
Nevertheless, or perhaps because of this, the last days of this long summer have been full of joy.
The Reverend Iain Greenshields, of the Scottish Church, spent last weekend in Balmoral.
On Saturday evening we had lunch together, and on Sunday we were with Charles and Anne.
It was a courtesy visit which I particularly enjoyed.
I told him of when I used to come to Balmoral as a child, about my horses, whose names I listed with satisfaction, and a little senile pride, one by one in chronological order.

For a great-grandmother of my age, having a good memory constitutes a victory over the laws of the Universe. Every date one remembers is like crossing a finishing line.

We also discussed Ukraine, and the issues of its Church. On the previous weekend the Reverend Martin Fair had visited me.

He found me in very good spirits, and I was pleased with his enviable physical form.

Certainly, this period spent in Balmoral was one of the most serene in recent years.

The change of climate has been good for me. I had my inner circle around me, including my own Angela Kelly, who is a friend and confidante to me, as well as being the official breaker of my shoes.

After she has tried them on, and has worn them for three days, they become like wings.

I have had frequent visits, from William and Kate with their children, Edward with Sophie, and Margaret's two children, who love me like a mother less capricious than the mum that befell them.

It was a typical summer in the country, with lots of walks, picnics and barbecues. Although I didn't participate in everything, it was as if I was there.

Tomorrow I have my meeting with the newly appointed Prime Minister Liz Truss. I've been preparing for days.

I'd like it if after seeing me she could tell the press that she found me bright, warm, welcoming.

Certainly an old woman, this word keeps bothering me, but always smart, with an open smile, and full of spirit.

It did not use to be like this, but everything has acquired a different value lately.
When it will finally happen, I would like to die here, among the beloved bricks of this castle.
The place where in August 1946 a young Royal Navy officer declared his love for me. And soon afterwards we declared ourselves to the world.
Here, unfortunately, is also where the news of your accident reached us.
But in this place, more often than in others, we were a happy family.
Together with the red deer, which one can spot early in the morning or in the evening when they come out to eat.
From these rooms I thought of you, of your destiny, and made peace with the people's princess.
And here, Diana, I have written other "posthumous" letters, which I do not intend to bury in the woods, near some copper beech planted by the Queen, as Edward II would do, but which will not be sent to unsuspecting recipients either. They are condemned, instead, to remain buried under the dust of the centuries, until some bookworm challenges time to a duel, time who at will can conceal or bring back to light.

Do not look for any last words, do not expect any revelations, or let alone some belated confessions. I will be as silent as one of the royal fish that enjoy the privilege of living under my rule.
And I will take my leave, without leaving answers that I would not have, and without formulating questions that would remain unanswered.
I really wouldn't want them to seal my whole life in a sentence like: “But has Sandy gone to the toilet?”
“After reassuring herself about her dog's physiological needs, Her Majesty Queen Elizabeth II peacefully fell asleep,” a palace note would read.

And don't compare me to the glorious Elizabeth the First. I am not sure that I have even a drop of her foul blood in my veins.
She aged into a frail, balding woman with black, rotten, malodorous teeth.
Her ladies took four hours a day to complete the ceremony of dressing and undressing the Queen, and she did not produce any offspring.
I, unlike her, leave behind three generations of future monarchs.
If you must find a resemblance, or some kind of affinity, let it be with the Great White Queen.

That little woman, no more than a hundred and fifty centimetres tall, and in prosperous times even more than a metre wide, Victoria Queen of Great Britain and

Empress of India, opulent ruler of a quarter of the population on the globe.
Her Majesty had those unmistakable, slightly squinting Hanoverian eyes, a tiny mouth that always tended to hang open a little, a receding chin and tiny feet. She was so petite that her favourite prime minister nicknamed her "The Fairy".
In truth, I would not like the idea of going down in history as a fairy.

And now we come to the last station. When will it be? A year from now, a day from now?
I don't know when, but soon I will be asked to get off.
When that happens, I would like a rainbow to appear in the sky.
My farewell from this life, which I believe I have honoured, and at times coloured in several shades, like my pastel green, indigo purple and hot pink caps.
But is that too much to ask?
For you Diana, death was the seal of your life, the final moment of a living legend, which needed a bitterly emphatic epilogue to become eternal.
That night, in the tunnel of Pont de L'Alma, you paid your dues, which history demands to open its doors wide and welcome the best travellers into its folds.
Those dearest to Heaven.

That will not be it for me.
I already know that the bell with its tolling will extinguish even the last glow.

A hundred years from now, with the exception of scholars and connoisseurs of the subject, no one will know in which century Elizabeth II reigned, without consulting an English history textbook.
My short eternity ends here, in this long winter of our silence.
Whether an invincible summer will follow, in the sunshine of the Lord's Prayer, I cannot know.
What say you, Diana?

Immortality has courted me during this long season, and each time it surprisingly seemed to announce the gift of a reign sine die.
But it was pure illusion.
“As long as there is the Endless Queen, we will cultivate the certainty of being in the world, feeling reassured about the present and less worried about the near future”, they incredibly wrote about me.
I smiled, and sometimes even I believed that I would last forever.
It seemed that Lady Death had forgotten about me.
So you know, Diana, the only thing that really matters in the end is how much we loved.
How strongly we used the axe that can break the sea of ice within us.
I think that when, between the byssus sheets of the royal bed, I bid farewell to myself and to the last Queen of a world that perishes with her, around the forest of faces that will accompany me on the threshold of time I will search my heart for the love that I have given, and the love that I have received.

I can only say thank you for that, England's Rose.

Like a silent film actress, I accepted to play the destiny of Elizabeth R which was assigned to me, in the second act of an epic film partly consumed by a diva who, professing to be chaste, shamelessly chastised her posterity.
And, in spite of myself I have honoured my mandate, albeit without being entitled to more than a few lines which were not already written in the plot of a human comedy of which I have been fleetingly a part for almost a hundred years of solitude.
I would do it all over again, and I will continue to do it.
But now, after a life humbled by the *raison d'état*, the only powerful memories are those that can evoke an emotion, an idea, or a passion.
Not those that are written in the script.
Before I retire from the scene and finally pass away, I would like to leave to the not-so-little prince who will succeed me a few superfluous recommendations.
To indulge my last vanities, more than to dictate my last will.

Be a good King, my son, but do not allow your humanity to take a back seat in the presence of the Crown, which will still hang over your head.
Take care of the Throne, but let it be placed at the service of men who write history, and build its path.
Thou shalt not hesitate to sacrifice it, without regret, if the sacrifice may benefit the journey of civilisation.

Be a good King, but on the battlefields of tomorrow remember your name, and do not forget to give thanks. Fight for the happiness of the planet, and of its inhabitants, and do not evade your promise to defend the faith, but be a defender of all faiths, and finally do not forget that by an inviolable law of nature you will be ineluctably alone when you reign, whenever you fall, and if you rise again.
Do not fear of being persecuted like a heretic, for a voice out of the chorus is the spice of life.
Do I seem to be rambling today?

She who is moving her uncertain steps towards the grand finale, may as well remove the mask. And break the silence.
For a few grave moments.
We had an empire to be guarded with the sword, now we have dignity to be guarded with peace.
Mary Stuart would have said: "Everything begins with a woman and ends with a woman."
I, on the other hand, think that everything can go on without me.
But if we are to remain seated where we are now, that obsolete chair will have to leave the palace rooms, and the King will have to show himself naked, and fill his soul with admiration and veneration, ever new and growing, towards the starry heavens above him and the moral law within us.
As Elizabeth watched over the borders of the Kingdom, the next King will have to watch over the boundless dreams of the people, that they may be beautiful dreams,

stand as a champion of happiness, his own and others', and stand as a sentinel of beauty, so that the world may save it, and save itself.

Otherwise the crown will roll from his head, shattering into a thousand pieces, as has already happened.

I have tired myself out, and tomorrow I will meet the new prime minister, but I have already told you that, haven't I?
At the end of this letter I can confess to you, Diana, that on the day of your farewell, the Queen tripped over the love the people showed for you.
Finding you again, as I wish I would, I would bow to the blade which you have been to me, with which I have poked at the embraces I have not given the silences I have not been able to break, and the waters I have not explored.
I wonder if you were aware, even remotely, of what you were building.

What about your mistakes? The pain you caused me?
And the pain we caused you?
But the pain is transformed, the disappointment and resentment inherent in its substance drain away in the flame of time, which medicates, and there remains a memory which can be manipulated, tamed, and put away somewhere.
Or nurtured, and even embellished.
It happens, and it happened even to your Queen.

I will not write down a date.

I wish it were the one of my last day in this vale of tears where I did not mind wintering.
My successor will write it in his own hand whenever he wishes, after the Lord Chamberlain has broken the Wand of Office, sanctioning the end of the reign of Elizabeth II.
God save the King.
Finally, God save the King.

Discover other success books realized by Edizioni &100 Marketing:

Scan the QR code and visit our website!

Do you want more info?

Contact us:

Telephone: 06 77207937

Mobile: 351 8081397

Email: info@edizionie100.com

Address: L.go K. Adenauer 8 – 00144, Rome
Via Bergamini 7 – 20122, Milan

From the same series:

Scrivi il tuo successo – Alessandro Gian Maria Ferri

Ho imparato – Massimo Imparato

Tu non puoi capire! – Marcella Loporchio

Trasforma i tuoi numeri in soldi – Salvatore Cortesini

Il cuore pulsante del consulente in saldo e stralcio – Pamela Righetti

L'infinito - Ester Giarrusso

I don't get Lucky, I make my own Luck– Alessandro Gradelli

Allenamento tailormade – Marco Colciaghi

Barista Ricco – Francesco Buompane

Da 0 a Franchising – Carlo Di Martino e Luca Siclari

Agente Immobiliare, la mia passione vincente – Dario Biato

La donna che sarò – Dress for Success Rome

Sicilia. Come eravamo, siamo, saremo - Emilio Aldo Maglie

Femmina dentro - Cristiana Himat Shakti Kaur

La badante perfetta... e non solo – Francesca Ciarlone

La forza del cambiamento è dentro di noi – Giulia Guarino

La rivoluzione dell'intelligenza artificiale – Gabriele Ponti

La vendita perfetta della tua casa – Iacopo Romi

Lava Self. Lo splendore in un gettone – Marco Radaelli

Le produttrici nel cinema italiano – Lisa Ferri

Le terre lontane - Robert Alin Dimofte

Professionista TOP – Giuseppe Tomasello

Sicuri Senza Glutine - Giancarlo D'Andrea

Soluzioni impresa – Thomas Coppola

Il Covid e gli appalti pubblici – Thelma Prestifilippo

Ultimo. Dall'ultimo banco alla finanza agevolata – Vito Virzi

Un diavolo per capello – Sergio Tirletti

Un imbranatissimo collezionista di attimi – Manlio Bitocchi

Una spremuta di me – Giorgio Gaetano Bottari

Uomini in fuga – Mimmo Leonetti

Da scugnizzo a sartorialist – Ciro Marigliano

Sogni – Armenio Del Picchia

L'ascolto che meriti, Il supporto che vuoi – Danyla De Vincentiis

Consapevolumilmente. Dal diario di bordo di un venditore – Vincenzo Parlavecchio

Kefa – Carmelo Caruso e Gianluigi Di Lorenzo

OMYA Studio e io – Cristina Bernard

Printed by Edizioni &100 Marketing.

Made in the USA
Las Vegas, NV
22 July 2024

92735178R00059